THE RETURN OF MAGIC

The country of Dowling had enjoyed a long and peaceful existence with many of its people practicing magic for the benefit of everyone in the Kingdom. Then one dark day it occurred to a depraved individual that with the power he had accumulated that he could be King and rule the whole Kingdom of Dowling. It so happened events that were about to take place made his depraved plans come to fruition.

The blistering sun beat relentlessly on the child as he lay fully exposed to the elements; where, his family had deemed he was to be placed. Tradition dictated that this particular abuse was to take place on each and every personage born of the Royal Blood. Fate on the other hand seldom cared about traditions but rather on different events; where good or bad mattered not.

As it happened the child moved and that movement drew the attention of a very hungry eagle, which, swooped down, seized the child and flew off with him. This unforeseen mishap left the Royal Family in deep mourning. Hence an all-out hunt for the future error of the kingdom was began; huntsmen from all over the Kingdom swore an oath to bring the prince home.

Meanwhile high over the swamps of the Eastern boarder of the Kingdom a hunter spied the eagle with the child and using his bow shot the eagle. The child fell from the clutches of the dead eagle into the putrefied water of the swamp. Never one to cry out for any reason the child after it hit the water; rolled over and proceeded to climb up on some long dead trees and lay down. The huntsman desperately in need of food proceeded to search for the eagle and the child it had dropped. When he found the eagle, he cut off the head and tying the legs together he hung it over his back; then, he searched for the child. Because it was getting dark and he had secured his next meal he turned and headed out of the swamp not wanting to be caught in it at night. He had determined that the child was probably dead anyway, having fallen that far, not worth looking further for; however, on his exit from the swamp he found the child. A boy of about five months old, black haired, and bruised all over. He had a bracelet on his arm with writing on it, but the huntsman could not read so he ignored it. Picking up the child he tramped through the swamp and into the bush where walking was easier and soon, he was home. Going inside he placed the child on his bed and went to prepare the eagle for supper.

During his meal he noticed the child looking at him so he threw a piece of the breast meat to him; but, later discovered it in the bed as all the child could do was suck on it. That convinced the huntsman to take the child deeper into the swamp where an old friend of his lived and would look after him. The very next day the huntsman took the child to his friend, who, some said was a witch and all stayed clear of her dwelling save him. Thus, it was that the child was raised by a witch and watched over by a huntsman. The witch fed the child and started training him in all sorts of casting spells, curses, potions and chants designed to make his life easier and she named him Savage because he looked like a Savage. So, for the next several years he grew and grew as a result of her ministrations and potions. No sooner had he drank one of the potions than the witch watched for any effects on him; then she had him drink another potion. The huntsman on one of his visits noticed how big the child had gotten and then how strong he was. The huntsman expressed concern for the child to the witch who told him to mind his own business. This bickering back and forth between the huntsman and the witch was what endeared them to each other and they both looked forward to it.

The witch was growing old and feeble by the time the child was 11 years of age and she said as much to the huntsman. He told her to use some of her potions to help and she said only the child should use them. Thus, it was that on his twelfth birthday the old witch died. The boy soon to be a man cleaned up around the cabin and dug a grave behind it to bury the only mother he could remember having. With the huntsman in attendance they said words over her and then proceeded to cover the grave. Savage asked the huntsman for his advice; to either continue living in the witch's home or leave and go with him. The huntsman said he would help Savage if he came with him so the boy went with him, could survive and become a man. They travelled for miles through the swamp and then came to a waterfall next to a pond. There they made camp and the boy watched as the huntsman proceeded to cut a branch off a tree that had two branches growing out of it. Then he peeled the branches and after making a small fire baked the branch in the fire to harden it. When he was finished, he had what looked like a fork and with it he went down to the water. At the edge of the pond he stood still until a fish swam by and he stabbed it with the fork then threw it up on the shore. Savage quickly grabbed the fish and watched as the huntsman made another stabbing plunge into an even bigger fish and threw it up on the shore. Having learned the art of fishing Savage was then shown how to clean and cook the fish; that, the huntsman said will ensure you will never starve.

For all the knowledge the witch had imparted to him nothing equaled the training the huntsman gave him. He was taught the different nuts to eat, and berries, plants and animals and birds that were available to him in the swamp. He was schooled in the art of using a staff for defense and the bow for hunting; such, were the teachings of the huntsman until he too died of a snake bite. Left on his own Savage at the age of sixteen was someone to take note of; being, six two about and one hundred and eighty pounds he was a big man. Black hair to his shoulders and down his back almost to his waist; black eyes like midnight that missed nothing, and a sharp wit defined him.

The Queen from the time of his birth was baron and the doctors considered the problem to be as a result of loosing a child. The King was so in love with her that even though the advisers told him to get rid of her and remarry for the sake of the Kingdom he would not. Then stories started to spread of a man who lived in the swamp, whose appearance was much like the King. This brought hope back to the Queen who while sitting eating with the King at the table heard the story. The King immediately saw the expression on the Queen's face and the flush of blood to her checks. The Queen asked him if it were possible that it could be her boy and he told her it was not. Undeterred by him she ordered a group of hunters to seek out the man in the swamp and bring him alive to the castle. She ordered them to in no way to harm him and so it was that Savage was found and returned to his real home.

The hunters brought him into the castle and up to the throne room; where he was placed before the King and Queen those in attendance could not tell the difference between him and the King save age. The King could hardly believe what he was seeing, and the Queen was overjoyed at seeing her son once again. Now everyone would have at this point said, how do we know this is the true son of our King? That was the question in everyone's mind until a bracelet on a string around Savage's neck was removed and handed to the King. The Queen of course recognized it right away and as the King read the inscription, it left no doubt about the young man's parents. The King read to our son Savage on his birth from Nathan and Stella, King and Queen of Dowling. Thus, Savage had returned home to a world as far removed from the swamp as day was from night but just as deadly.

Savage was taught to read and write and do sums; however, he did not care much for school. His main interest was in armed combat at which he excelled; especially, with the sword and bow. It was during this time that he met a young lady who also enjoyed shooting the bow and together many days were spent hunting together. It was during one of these trips that they heard people talking about killing the King and Queen and taking over the Kingdom. Intrigue and deceit were rampant in the Kingdom at that time and Savage and Sally were trapped in the knowledge they had just gained. Together they went to the King and Queen and told them what they had heard; however, because they named people the King and Queen trusted they dismissed them out of hand. As a result, Savage and Sally decided to take steps to ensure they themselves would not be killed as members directly associated with the Royal Family. Savage made a map of the surrounding Kingdom, showing the landscapes and swamps, stretches of forest and the large swamp from where he came and was raised. He made sure Sally was fully aware and knowledgeable of his map and his teachings. He then started taking certain of his soldiers, members he was friends with and run practices of, swordplay, bow shooting; trapping of animals and what to eat and what not to eat in the swamp. This planning seemed pointless to many of his friends until the revolt by the members of the upper-class people who paid mercenaries to kill all the members of the Royal Family and those who supported them. Many people died during that first three months and those that Savage, and Sally had trained escaped to the big swamp. There the revolutionaries were unable to track them and they turned back to the castle.

During the revolution one evil man Tomilson took charge and set himself up as the new King; however, he had no Queen and he sent his troops out to find the best-looking woman they could find. During their search they found a young woman who was beautiful and single, so they took her to the new King. He liked her and married her even though she did not approve, but that made no difference to him; he told her marry me or I will have your entire family killed. So she agreed to marry him. Tomilson was a very cruel and demanding King; having an army of mercenaries to back him up he stripped the country of all its treasures. It became clear to him though that the one thing he could not do was kill the holdouts in the swamp no matter what he tried. It was during this time that Savage himself was taken prisoner by a group of men and women who had surrounded a small cottage near the swamp. To their surprise they found four men and two women in the cottage; so, after tying them up they started torturing them to learn who they were.

Shortly after the torturing had started one of the women broke down and told all she knew, which, put Savage and his best leaders in dire peril. The torturers sent word to the new King to tell him who they had captured and how much they wanted as a reward. The King dispatched a troop of soldiers to take possession of the captives and to kill the men and women who held them captive.

So it was that on the eighth day of the eighth month at eight o-clock in the evening the Kings soldiers slaughtered all the men and women at the rendezvous. The captives were unchained and washed clean then fed and tied up again as the soldiers had been ordered to do. It was about that time that fate again took a hand and during the night a group of Savage's men set the captives free. The guards and soldiers were so tired from their long trip fell fast asleep and heard nothing of the escape. Savage had words with Sally and then he went back into the soldier's camp where she again retied him and left. In the morning, the soldiers were at first confused then infuriated at the loss of all but one of the captives. As a result the guards of the night were killed for falling asleep. The leader of the soldiers ordered them to march for hours and would not let any of them rest until noon. He never once questioned who the only captive was but took heart that he had at least one captive to show the King. Days passed and on the fifth day the soldiers could finally see their objective in the distance. Now it became easier to march along as they were in the home stretch and looking forward to their sweethearts and food and drink and rest. Little did they realize that as soon as they had accepted the job of bringing back the captives their doom had already been confirmed by the King. He had ordered the palace guard to execute all the soldiers who had gone with the Captain that morning so long ago; more than twenty men.

Savage was turned over to the Palace Guard and then locked in a cell; he could hear the Palace Guards saying how fortunate he was to be the only one left alive. Several days later he learned the fate of the soldiers who had brought him here to the Palace. He had been questioned by the King's men to find out if he knew the swamp and if he knew the leader of the rebels who lived there. Savage provided information that only one of his people would know thereby proving he was from the swamp and the King's men would trust him. Several of the King's men had gone into the swamp using Savage's limited map and were alright. The King was overjoyed and told his men to tell Savage that if he could direct them on how to capture the swamp people then he would be greatly rewarded. Thus, it was that the King and Savage the leader of the swamp people found themselves entering the swamp together as allies. Never had an army as great as this one ever entered the swamp for fear of quicksand, snakes, fever and leaches and all manner of other dangers. Saying nothing of the swamp people who were known to kill strangers and sink their bodies into the swamp never to be seen again. It was now the 10th of the month and just about all the army was committed to the swamp. The King in the meantime kept Savage under careful observation at the cook's wagon, where he was employed pealing potatoes, carrots and doing the cooks biding.

Sally during the night had brought a bunch of different leaves and roots and other items like nuts and gave them to Savage, who as the cook prepared the evening meal, added them to the stew. He was careful not to eat any of it, claiming a sick stomach and having thrown up earlier. The cook had noticed him being sick behind the wagon but had said nothing, so he never made Savage eat the stew. That night for supper more than sixty men at arms, all mercenaries ate the stew and died in their sleep including the cook. When the order to march was given the next morning more than a third of the King's army were dead. Men searched for a reason but found nothing, while Savage and one other man who like Savage had been sick were all that remained alive. The King's men questioned them both to no avail and finally the King said let us proceed as planned; the swamp will take care of the dead. For a time, the King's men could hear the birds and alligators and other animals as they fed, which made them unsure of their present quest. The King on the other hand took the loss of some of his men as a sign he was getting close to catching and destroying the rebels. Little did he realize that his ranks were being infiltrated with rebels; men willing to chance all for a chance to kill the King.

     During the Kings absence from the court and his men, the nobles, became quite brave some saying the King was not the true King. Others spread rumors of a great battle that took place in the swamp and the rebels were defeated, others said the King was defeated. So, it went for days on end rumor after rumor and the ladies who were aware of them started to seek alliances with men who had riches and lands. Each one acted in complete secrecy so that should the King be successful no-one could say they were unfaithful. These alliances suited the gentry well, as they, had to sit back and watch as the prettiest and smartest women were claimed by the King's men. Love never once entered the minds or actions of the King or his men, who were nothing more than animals in men's clothes. Then as time went by the alliances become stronger and more visible to everyone and all the people prayed that the rebels would win a great victory against superior odds.

On September the 12th at approximately 9am the King's men encountered what they thought was the rebel forces. So excited had the King become that he ordered his frontline soldiers to attack, which was exactly what the rebels wanted. The soldiers raced forward and found themselves sinking in quicksand, which in the panic that ensued caused the death of nearly all the soldiers in the front line. The remaining men fell back and were being killed one by one, by arrows shot from cover. The King ordered his men to retreat which they attempted to do when they were met by rebels shooting arrows into them. The King and his men now surrounded dug in, in an attempt to defend themselves from attack. As the days wore on starvation, snake bites, fever and arrows claimed more and more men, until desperate the last remaining men and the King made a breach in the rebel lines and ran for their very lives. Many men whom the King left behind died not from rebel arrows but ignorance and snake bites. A runner was dispatched by the King to the palace; ordering the elite palace guard to be ready to repel the rebels who were supposedly pursuing him and his men. Of the where abouts of Savage and the rebels the King knew not; but if he could find him, the King vowed to kill him slowly over an open fire pit.

The in desparation the King and his remaining men burst free of the swamp and raced to the palace; where many of the alliances that had been made; were dissolved discreetly. However, some alliances were maintained even as the soldiers returned because many never returned; having succumbed to injuries sustained in the swamp. Meanwhile others returned but had high fevers and strange afflictions on there bodies which made them unable to have children. Prince Savage harassed the King's Guard all the way back to the palace and then set up a siege against the place. Prince Savage knew that fresh water and food were short in the Palace and with that knowledge he settled in for a short siege.

One day while Prince Savage and Sally were eating and discussing the effects the siege was having on the palace a courier arrived. He was met and issued into the tent where Savage and Sally were sitting; then, he informed them that the King during a fit of rage had tripped and fell over the parapet and died. The courier told them the city was theirs and the King's Guard were prepared to acknowledge Savage as the true King of the Land. Savage lifted the siege and with his army of rebels approached the front gate of the palace and demanded it be opened. The gate of the palace was opened and for the first time in years men and women entered the palace where most of them had been born. Prince Savage proceeded to the throne room where the body of the evil King lay in state and ordered the body to be removed and burned. Then assuming the scepter and being seated on the throne of his father, the King's Guard and the revels swore fealty to the new King save one. Unobserved in the background stood a very unlikely enemy of the King and as the celebrations continued, he silently disappeared.

Weeks went by and King Savage was now being pressed to take a bride so the Kingdom could have a successor in the future. Reluctant as he was, he did fancy Sally; she was a warrior, friend and confidant; yet he could not see her as soft and yielding. While looking around he could find no other damsel that quickened his senses; so, he thought he would try to get to know Sally better. He decided to take walks in the garden with her and discuss the flowers and birds they saw as well as her plans.

King Savage and Sally were on such a walk and had taken a seat just to rest a bit when a bolt from a crossbow pierced Sally's chest and pinned her to the bench. The King rolled clear and into the bushes that grew close by; then gaining his feet he ran to gain a position behind the killer. Having successfully approached the killer from the rear the King grabbed him and swung him around, exposing, the face of his best friend. At least that was what Savage had believed up till now; however, he had his guards take his friend away and chain him in the dungeon.

King Savage for all his twenty-one years on the earth had learned lessons that would have crippled most men. He learned what it was like to lose a mother and father; also, to be abandoned in a swamp. He remembered the lessons taught to him by the witch who he thought was his mother, and the loss of the woodsman his friend. Then his being ripped from the swamp and being claimed as a long-lost son. The endless hours of training in how to eat, speak, drink, act and dress; not counting sword drills, map reading and school.

Then the death of his true father and mother and a run to the swamp once again to save his life along with many others. The relentless attacks he witnessed upon the poor of the Kingdom by the Evil King and his guards. This then was the background and training King Savage had acquired before the age of 21 years. Most men would have given up, some would have killed themselves and others would have become bitter and twisted. Not so King Savage he dedicated himself to his people, seeing to them helped building new homes, getting children into schools and educating his soldiers. Not everyone was pleased at first but as time went on everyone in the Kingdom became aware of just how much better off they really were and how miserable their King really was.

King Savage decided one afternoon to take a group of his soldiers and camp in the swamp, then have a wild pig hunt. He got everyone dressed in woodsman get-up with green pants, shirts, leather boots and long bows. His intent was to teach them that not every woodsman they met was dim witted; in fact, many were quite smart. They had walked for several miles when one of them spotted a pig; at which everyone shot an arrow, needless to say they all missed. The King laughed out loud and then apologized at which everyone burst out laughing. It was then that a scream was heard floating over the swamp and the squeal of a pig could be heard as well. Savage and his men quickly advanced through the swamp to where the screams came from and they found a large snake wrapped around a pig and a young woman trying to save the pig. The men quickly killed the snake and set the pig free; then the King approached the woman and found himself enthralled with her beauty.

Susan was taken by the King and his men back to their camp where they secured the pig in a pen for safety. Then after a hasty meal they all went to bed except the King and the young woman who wanted to thank him and his men for saving her and her pig. As they sat at the fire that night a bond was formed between them and even though no words of love passed either of their lips that night, love formed in both their hearts. In the morning, the men arose to a King who seemed to have come alive again and a young woman who could not do enough for him. It was very apparent to all in camp that the King was infatuated with the woman and she with him. The hunting party was quickly turned from hunting pigs to one of celebration and rejoicing which after several days saw them all sated.

Savage bid his men and the young woman return with him to the palace which they all did. The King had several ladies in waiting greet the woman called Susan and assist her in bathing and dressing for the evening meal. When she was dressed and cleaned up with her hair done and nails cleaned, she looked like a Queen. Seated as she was Savage could only stare down the long table to where she sat talking to members of the household. It was as everyone new and understood the custom of Savage to have his servants after the meal was served to be seated with him at the table to eat. He made no difference in any of their stations and talked openly to each one. During one of their conversations a stable boy asked Savage if he intended to marry the woman called Susan and he said yes. That is he said if she will accept me as I am a King and nobleman, ruler of all this Kingdom and the swamp.

Savage pledged his troth to Susan, and she asked him pointedly if he was aware of what his proposal really meant. The King was at once surprised and cautious as he asked her for an explanation. Susan took him into the garden where she demonstrated her skill at growing different plants and trees; then as she changed her mood, she killed several plants just by touch. She had watched Savage's face while she did these things and noticed how intently he had observed her different abilities. When she had finished Savage without saying a thing reached out to the dead plants and touching them, they sprang back to life.

It was Susan's turn to be astounded and sitting on a bench later in the garden with the King she realized he was the young man raised by the swamp witch. She was a distant relative of Susan's and she had many of the witch's talents; Savage said he felt at home with her and she accepted his proposal of marriage. Everyone in the Kingdom was overjoyed for Savage and they planned a great celebration that to this day has not been equaled. The whole Kingdom was present, and the wedding took place on a hill in front of the palace itself outside. King Savage and Queen Susan went among the people thanking them for their kindness and best wishes and the people responded with love and devotion. A year later a pair of twin girls were born in the palace and each exhibited ability in magic; like levitation, plant growth, talking to birds and animals.

This then started the return of magic in the land that had been exterminated by the evil King. Savage did not realize that the swamp witch that raised him and the huntsman who trained him did so in the hope he would be the one to rejuvenate magic in the Kingdom. They did not however place all their eggs in one basket as an old couple in the swamp were raising a girl to do the same thing. Never did they ever think that, that same girl and boy would meet, fall in love, and marry. Their offspring were the delight of the Kingdom and all who saw the girls were impressed by their beauty. Then another child was born only this time it was a boy who from the day of his birth proved to be a handful. He by the time two months had passed was able to teleport, levitate, read minds and crush cups with his mind. The Queen expressed her concerns to Savage, saying he, their son could become dangerous to the people caring for him, if he was not controlled. Savage did not like the idea of controlling his son; however, for the safety of everyone he placed a spell of control over him. Then during the next sixteen years that spell was never reversed; in fact, it was totally forgotten about. Trevor was an extraordinary young man and his sword instructor commented many times to the King about his ability to use a sword. His mother the Queen had him instructed in dance, cooking and most of all service to others.

During those sixteen years Trevor was the delight of the Kingdom, a powerful athlete and swordsman. His ability to dance and sing always infatuated the young maidens in the towns and his mother delighted in eating the meals he made for her on weekends. He had one habit that if his Royal Family knew about, they would have put a stop to; that of hunting in the great swamp. Sometimes bad things happen when you are not where your suppose to be; and as it happened during just such a hunt Trevor slipped and fell into water deep enough to have covered a spear that pierced his chest. Thankfully, it went in high enough to miss his heart; yet it went in deep enough to cause severe bleeding. As the young man staggered through the swamp, he became confused as to which way to go and after quite a long trek he collapsed against a tree. He must have been hallucinating because as he lay there, he could have sworn he saw a very large bird of some type land near him and turn into a woman.

At that point Trevor knew he was dying because he was seeing things that were not real and then he got the impression of flying, but he had no wings and he told the woman so. Days past and Trevor lay at death's door; his fever was very high and a terrible infection was killing him. The fairies had tried almost everything they knew of except the disenchantment spell which only the oldest could use. Fear gripped the fairies for if the spell did not work it would kill the one who cast it. Such was the dilemma they faced, save the young man or lose their elder, how could anyone make that decision.

History records a time when the swamp fairies faced a great decision; but before any action could be taken fate stepped in land the young man's fever broke and his father's spell was broken as well. Now Trevor could fight the infection with all his strength and power and his recovery was nothing short of a miracle. The elder entered his room to find him up dressed and hungry. She smiled at him and sent a thought out to him which he responded to in kind; that totally shocked her and then she said come with me please. His introduction to the swamp fairies was piece meal at best as many were asleep, and others were on duty watching the swamp for intruders. Many times, they had seen him hunting and always he left and did not come back for quite a while; however, when he started towards their home, they called in Lana to turn him away. It was her he saw as he lay against the tree and it was her that carried him home to safety and help. Never had any of the fairies helped the humans. Trevor proved to be more than he was and during his stay with the fairies he danced with some, made breakfast for others and served wine to others. Trevor was true to his upbringing, a profoundly good man and the fairies all agreed that if he swore never to reveal them, he could leave.

Thus, fully recovered Trevor left the swamp and returned home to a very worried father and mother. The King was the first to realize Trevor had changed; things seemed to appear and then disappear whenever he was around. Trevor's mother got a fright when a grey wolf stocked her across the lawn, but as Trevor approached it fled, then from nowhere Trevor gave her some beautiful flowers. Many were the times when good things happened to those in need and always Trevor was around. It was not until one day late in the afternoon when beautiful woman met Trevor on the landing outside his room. Right away Trevor knew it was

Lana and there must be trouble, or she would not have come. She spoke of wonder and love and not being able to sleep for thinking and searching for him day and night until she had to see him. She found out from the elder who he really was and where to find him but warned her that his feelings might not be as strong as hers.

Trevor hearing her confession of love took her hands in his and kissed her; because he felt as she did, and he said that when they were together, they were at peace and when apart there was always something missing. He escorted her down to the throne room where his father and mother were talking about him and the changes, they had observed in him. He knocked and pushing open the door with his mind walked in with Lana at his side.

The King and Queen were stunned when he closed the door with his power and then he addressed them in their minds. They had never felt such power and then Trevor spoke, introducing Lana and telling them of his accident and her saving his life. He also, mentioned the high fever that broke his containment spell, and his love of Lana and their plans. The King and Queen were skeptical of their love but said nothing preferring to wait and see; after all Lana had saved their son's life and maybe that was why he thought he loved her.

Trevor took Lana on a tour of the Palace and even down into the chambers below the Palace where the evil King had many people tortured. It was during that tour that something called out to Lana and she froze stock still and listened. Then Trevor heard the cry and together they proceeded to search for its origin. This was no easy task as they had to climb over boxes and cases of different food stuffs and then move some heavy war machines. Still after all that, the cry continued to come from that one direction and by now Trevor and Lana were fully engrossed in the search. Stopping to catch a breath and take a brake Trevor said, Lana what on earth do you think the cry is? She replied, if it is what I think it is my people have searched for it for generations. Trevor said really what is it? Lana replied, an incredibly special sword of hardened silver with a gold handle and precious stones inlaid on it. Across the blade itself is an inscription that only one of pure blood can wield this sword and live. The sword was enchanted centuries ago and can speak if people of magic are near.

Trevor having recovered after their break started moving some of the heavier crates when he wound up facing a blank wall. Lana said oh! Look Trevor here is some writing, and together they bent forward to read what was written; "Beware the Jaws of Death", that was all it said. Together they stood and looked at the wall and then Trevor said I might as well see what is behind the veil and he stepped forward. Totally unprepared was he as he stepped forward something seized his right arm with pearly teeth that sank to the bone and the pain was terrible. Then he realized he was being pulled forward into the darkness, and only for Lana he would have been lost. Lana sprang into action, grabbing Trevor by his left arm and pulled him free, then she sent a force of death after the head with the teeth.

Screams of rage and pain and regret issued from the veil and then thrashing sounds then silence rained. Lana turned her attention to Trevor who was bleeding badly from a right arm and hand that under normal circumstances would have had to be removed. He was badly hurt, and Lana cast a healing spell on him and gradually he relaxed, and his arm began to heal. It took maybe half an hour for Trevor to regain use of his hand and arm and then turning to the veil he and Lana saw only an old wooden door. The cry that had brought them this far still sounded only now it was coming from behind the door.

Trevor at this point said something that was to be forever true, he said "My Castle, My Love, My Blood", and with that he opened the door with his mind. The door stood for an instant in place then it was forced off its hinges and flung across the inner room. There were several rooms each holding incredible magics that everyone in the Kingdom had considered lost. The creature that had guarded it was found curled in a ball in a corner dead. Trevor had the rooms emptied and their contents placed on long tables in the anti-room of the castle; there anyone who remembered how to use any of the magics could have them. A notice was sent out for the people to come and they did from miles around, some new and claimed some of the magics while others left disappointed.

Near the closing time of the third day an old lady came and looked over the magics and she hummed a tune as she surveyed them. Then she turned and went down the opposite side of the tables that held the magics and stopped at an old rusted sword and scabbard. She bent her head and tears flowed down her cheeks as she stood staring at it; then she straightened up and looked right at Trevor. Trevor felt the question even as it was asked, and he responded with; as you wish mother. This response although totally unexpected thrilled the old lady and as she stood there she turned into a beautiful fairy. Lana who had been watching another late comer turned and seeing her for the first time bowed her head to the floor and stayed so until told to rise; at that point Lana joined Trevor and approached the Fairy Queen. When they reached a distance of mere feet from the Queen, she stopped them and stated: You are Prince Trevor, son of King Savage and Queen Stella of the House of Dowling, born twenty-four years ago is that right? Trevor said yes, why do you ask? It was then that the Fairy Queen told him and Lana a tale so unbelievable they could hardly understand its portent.

The Queen said many years ago a murder took place in the swamp and the King of the Fairies was no more. I was left to rule the Fairies from that point until now. Back then my council and I decided that a new King of the Fairies should be revealed from the old King's bloodline. Our problem was simple really, how or should I say who was of the Royal Bloodline. We searched for years until an old manuscript was found that had traced the King's heritage up to the present day. In that heritage was mentioned a man who had decided to live his life in the swamp; you I believe called him the huntsman.

Trevor was stunned at that statement; but he was due for another more startling revelation. The Queen went on to say the huntsman had a wife and everybody called her the witch of the swamp. Together they had a daughter your mother Trevor, who never knew her true mother as she was raised by an old couple near the swamp as planned. Trevor said that then would leave me as a direct descendant of the Fairy King would it not? The Queen said yes, but to prove it we must consult the crying sword. No one can touch the sword for fear of dying, unless they are a true blood; do you want to test that theory Trevor?

Lana stepped forward and said Trevor it is not necessary for you to prove or disprove the theory. She went on to say I will still love you regardless and having said that she stepped back. Trevor saw the tears in her eyes and the excitement in the Fairy Queen's eyes and it left him overwhelmed with the decision he faced.

Trevor was cautious but young and full of himself so he said let's try your theory; fully confident that he could cope with what was to come. Together the three of them went down along the tables until they reached the old rusted sword and then stopped. Trevor said is this the famous crying sword everyone has searched for and are afraid of at the same time, and the Queen said yes. Fine Trevor said let's prove once and for all this theory of yours and without hesitation he reach over, picked up the sword and stood staring at them.

At first nothing happened and then a force of energy surged through his body which dropped him to his knees. Trevor's hands began to tremble and then the rust on the sword fell off to reveal the gold handle with precious stones in it. The blade shone its brilliance as Trevor's countenance began to change. Lana seeing him in trouble reached forward to help him but was forced back by an invisible force.

The Fairy Queen watched with fear for Trevor in her eyes, and hope in her heart. Trevor tried to release the sword, but it clung to him and then Trevor's clothes started to change. He had a severe pain in his back and then two beautiful wings sprouted from his back as his clothes changed to light green pants and vest with shoes the color of the forest. The Fairy Queen gasped and bowed herself to the ground before him, acknowledging his superiority. Once again, the Fairy peoples had a King and they would not have to hide from the likes of men and longer. Trevor told the Queen to rise and taking Lana's hand he said I guess things are not as they used to be and then his father King Savage and his Mother entered the room. Up to now King Savage said the blood line of the fairy King was considered lost to the world of magic. He went on to say I am proud to say my son has been proven to be of the true blood and is the successor of the King of the Fairies. King and Queen declared a truce between the Fairies and Man Kind putting to rest the age-old vendettas.

The Fairy Queen waved her wand and she turned again into the old woman they had first seen at the tables. She turned and said please come to the Fairy Circle on the occasion of the next full moon and then she was gone. Trevor looked at Lana and asked if she knew what the request was all about, but she had no idea. It was not a long time to wait as the next full moon was only three days hence and as requested Trevor and Lana were present. All the Fairies from far and wide were present, seated around the circle when the Fairy Queen came down the path from her home and entered the circle. Everyone present were surprised that she entered the circle, this had not happened in centuries. Then as the whispers and talking died down the Queen started to speak saying, the time has come for me to pass my crown to someone younger and stronger of spirit. Everyone protested even Trevor but the Queen went on to say my time as Queen ended when my husband was killed and at that time I told all of you that I would remain as your Queen until a true blood was found and became King. That has taken place and I would like to introduce to all of you our new King of the Fairies Trevor of Dowling. There were cheers and crying and thanksgiving that a true King had been found. Then the Queen removed her crown and placed it on the ground in the center of the circle and said, "All may try, Come who may, But only one will be Queen today". Then she bowed out of the circle and stood and watched as fairy after fairy tried and failed to pick up the crown. Finally, only one remained and that was Lana and she hung back for fear the crown would reject her as well. Then encouraged by all she stepped forward and reached down and picked up the crown placing it on her head. Traditionally the King of the Fairies always took the Queen of the Fairies as his wife, and in this case, it was plain to see that they were in love even before the choices of fate had been made.

And so, it was that!!!

King Trevor took Lana of the swamp fairies as his Queen an as far as anyone knows they still live in the swamp. It is said that even today men can enter the swamp, but there are areas where they can not go.